Cold Night, Brittle Light

Richard Thompson • Henry Fernandes

ORCA BOOK PUBLISHERS

It was cold outside — probably the coldest day of the whole winter — but it was warm in the kitchen. We were expecting Daddy home from town any time. Mom and I were baking gingerbread men. Grandmother was knitting. And Grandfather was remembering . . .

"Watching you sitting there knitting, Aggie," Grandfather said to Grandmother, "reminds me of the winter Aunt Doreen came to visit from the city. It was cold that winter, too, and Doreen didn't like the cold. She was sure we were all going to freeze to death.

"Aunt Doreen set to knitting wool socks and shawls and sweaters for everybody. Well, the old girl worked herself into a knitting frenzy. She arrived on Tuesday night. By Thursday her bedroom was right full. By Friday afternoon you couldn't get into the parlour for woollen goods. By noon on Saturday, the girls' bedroom and the cellar were full. Thank goodness the weather broke that afternoon, or she'd have filled up the kitchen.

"It was around Christmas that year that John Botherton had that bit of bother with his cows. He got to worrying that his chickens might freeze. He wanted to bring them into the house, but his wife Lucy said no, they'd drive her crazy with their cackling if he did. So he moved them into the barn with the cows, figuring the cows would keep them warm.

"Well, the chickens were fine in there with all those big warm bodies, but the cows didn't fare as well. The constant cackling and squawking and bluck, bluck, bluck . . . it got so bad it spoiled their milk.

"Next morning when John went out to do the milking, he saw that the milk was coming out all thick and yellowish. He stuck his finger in the milk pail and took a taste. Darned if those cows weren't giving egg nog!"

I smiled at Grandfather's story, but I was starting to worry — where was Daddy? I went to the window and melted a hole with my breath so I could see out. I could see his tracks heading off, but no Daddy coming back.

"You figure he's okay?" I asked.

"Oh, yeah, he'll be fine, Chrissy," said Grandfather. "This isn't what you'd really call cold. Remember Aggie, that same Christmas you made some gingerbread men? It was so cold that when you pulled them out of the oven, they took one look and crawled right back in, locking the door behind them."

It was almost dark now, and still no sign of Daddy.

"I'm worried, Mom," I said.

"Your dad will be just fine, Chrissy," said my mom. "You set the table now, and I'll put the stew on to heat for supper."

I did that, and then I went to look out again. I watched and watched. I kept imagining that one dark shape — and then another dark shape — was moving, and it was Daddy coming. But it wasn't Daddy — just trees standing out along the fence line.

Then suddenly the sky was full of light. It was like someone was rolling out a bolt of shot silk across the sky, and giving it a shake from time to time, making the colours shimmy and dance against the black.

"The Northern Lights!" I cried. "They're beautiful! Mom! Grandfather! Grandmother! Come look!"

They all came over and took turns looking out through the little peephole in the frost, and ooohing! and aaahing! because the light was so wonderful.

I watched and watched until Mom finally said, "We'd best go ahead and eat. I'll keep some warm for your dad."

Over supper Grandfather was still remembering . . .

"Your grandmother's fresh baking was one of the things that kept us going that winter, but even home baking had its dangers. One afternoon, she was baking pies and she ran out of raisins, so she sent me over to the neighbour's to borrow some. I got bundled up and headed out into the cold. Your grandmother stood in the door waving to me as I went. Without thinking, I turned and blew her a kiss. Well, it was so cold that the kiss froze into a solid lump before it got halfway to the house."

"It fetched me such a whack on the forehead that it knocked me senseless for the better part of the day," said Grandmother. "I never did get those pies done."

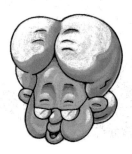

"The cold that winter caused a few problems for the folks in town, too," said Grandfather. "It was so cold that when people's breath came out it froze solid. A person had to break off one breath and throw it down on the ground before he could take another one. Soon there were lumps of frozen breath all over the streets. It wasn't long before you could hardly move downtown for the piles of breath every place you turned.

"Finally, they were forced to bring in two tanker cars full of Tabasco sauce from the city. People brought watering cans down to the station. The station agent filled them up with that peppery concoction, and everybody — even the mayor and his wife — was out there sprinkling Tabasco sauce on those hunks of frozen breath. Well, you know how hot Tabasco sauce is. As soon as it hit the piles of breath, they fizzed into steam and blew away.

"Of course, come spring the gutters were running with hot sauce mixed with mud. If you stepped in a puddle, it ate right through the bottom of your shoe."

I was listening to Grandfather and looking out when I noticed something strange. The Northern Lights were still shining as bright as ever, but they weren't shimmying and dancing like before. They looked like they were painted on the sky. I called Mom and Grandfather and Grandmother to come and look.

"Must be colder than I figured," said Grandfather. "The Northern Lights are frozen solid. I only saw that happen once before."

"It's Daddy!" I cried out. "Daddy's coming! I see him."

When Daddy came in, I ran over and swung the door shut so the cold wouldn't come in with him. But I shut it a bit too hard I guess because . . .

"Shhhh!" said Grandfather. "Listen!"

I could hear a faint tinkling sound. It got louder. Then it was like we were in the middle of an earthquake in a window factory. There were tinkling and cracking and breaking sounds all around us. The lights went out. Then, as suddenly as it had started, the noise stopped.

"What happened?" I cried. "Why did the lights go out?"

"It's okay," said Grandfather. "It's nothing serious. The Northern Lights get real brittle when they're frozen like that. All it takes is one loud noise and they just shatter into little pieces."

I ran to the window and looked out. The sky was empty black except for the stars, but there were slivers and shards of light scattered all over the yard.

"We've had our power cut off," said Grandfather. "I expect one of those shards of Northern Light must have sliced through the electric lines as it was falling."

"You come and have some supper," said my mom to Daddy. "I'll find some candles."

"Coming," said Daddy. "Hey, Chrissy, I got you a new book when I was in town."

"You'd better not start your new book tonight, Chrissy," said Mom. "You'll ruin your eyes reading in this dim light."

After Daddy had his supper, the grownups sat in front of the fire drinking coffee. I went to the window and scraped a clean spot so I could see out again. Looking out at the yard littered with scraps of light, I had an idea.

I tiptoed into the pantry and grabbed the big wicker basket. I got all bundled up and went out into the yard. Very carefully, I collected a whole basketful of bits of frozen Northern Light.

I took the basket into the house and laid the broken chunks on three cookie sheets. I put the cookie sheets in the oven, and I waited.

After a few minutes, I could see a glimmer around the edges of the oven door. "Mom! Daddy!" I called. "Grandmother! Grandfather! Come see!"

When the family came into the kitchen, I opened the oven door.

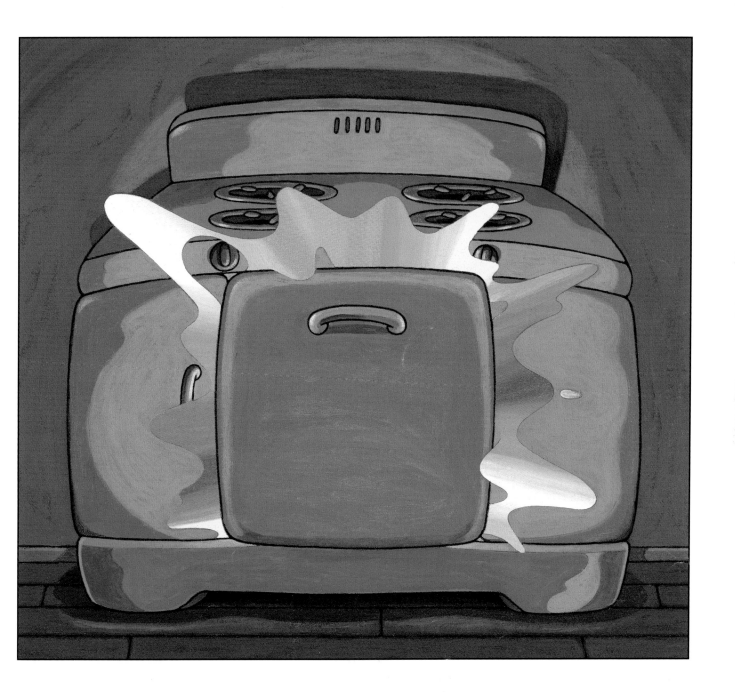

Light came rippling out of the stove. It wafted up to the ceiling and came together there, floating and shimmering, filling the whole room with its brightness.

"Sit down, Grandmother," I said. "I'll get your knitting."

So, by the light of the Northern Lights swimming lustrous on our kitchen ceiling, Grandmother sat knitting and I sat reading my new book. Mom got out her mending. Daddy fell asleep in his chair.

And Grandfather kept on remembering . . .

"It was so cold that winter that my shadow froze to the side of the house and I couldn't get it off till spring . . ."

To Maggee and Jesse
R.T.

To Mom, with love
H.F.

Text copyright © 1994 Richard Thompson
Illustration copyright © 1994 Henry Fernandes

Publication assistance provided by The Canada Council

Canadian Cataloguing in Publication Data
Thompson, Richard, 1951 –
Cold night, brittle light

ISBN 1-55143-009-6
II. Fernandes, Henry.   II. Title.
PS8589.H53C6 1994   jC813'.54   C94-901125-0
PZ7.T56Co 1994

Design by Christine Toller
Printed and bound in Hong Kong

Orca Book Publishers
PO Box 5626, Station B
Victoria, BC V8R 6S4
Canada

Orca Book Publishers
#3028, 1574 Gulf Road
Point Roberts, WA 98281
USA